Adam the Forsaken

Book 1 in

Tales of Extraordinary Beings

Adam Thomas Applebaum

ISBN: 0692224238
ISBN-13: 978-0692224236 (Adam Thomas Applebaum)

DEDICATION

This book is dedicated to my YouTube fans and friends throughout the world. I hope you all live fulfilled lives and continue to support my efforts to immortalize myself through the content I produce. Additionally, I would like to thank Andrea Genreau for being the first one on the list of buyers for this book and user Teodoro Hernandez III for contributing funds through Kickstarter towards perfecting this book to what it is now. I wish to extend thanks to anyone who has purchased this book. Thanks also to Hiroki Shima for agreeing to translate this into Japanese for me upon its completion.

CONTENTS

ACKNOWLEDGMENTS

Adam the Forsaken is a fictional book about a cat boy who starts out living a relatively typical life. However, the average life slowly goes from bad to worse as he gets older. The Book takes place from the year Nineteen-Ninety C.E. to Two Thousand C.E.
During this time, cell phones were gaining popularity. If smartphones existed at all, very few people had them. This book is not intended for children or the faint of heart due to descriptions of murder, violence, and abuse. This is a cautionary tale designed to satirically shed some light on real and fictitious issues of our time. Some names may or may not have been changed for legal reasons, and nothing written in this book should be taken as a threat to the world or an allegory to a real-life murder plot, nor do I condone any illegal activity. Any likenesses to people, places, or actual events are coincidental. I hope you enjoy this book.

-   ADAM THOMAS APPLEBAUM.

1 THE BIRTH OF ADAM THE FORSAKEN

The Tale Begins

Adam the Forsaken was born in San Dimas Hospital. His mother, Joanne, and father David now had a son to love and traditionally inherit what the father owned. David is a health physicist, and Joanne was at the time a microbiologist. Adam has two older sisters Cara and Tara. Cara and Tara were a little over eight and one-half years old when Adam was born. Tara and Cara had begged for a long time to have a baby brother.

Although their wish was granted, there is a meaning behind the famous saying, "Be careful what you wish for because you just might get it."

Yes, for a good portion of Adam's infancy Cara and Tara enjoyed taking care of him as they would a baby doll, but the novelty was not to last. Adam was a curious one and would occasionally get into their belongings once he'd learned to walk.

If one had asked his father, he might have said: "The adversity in those early years was keeping his older sisters from killing him."

Amusing as it is to imagine that, the story truly begins at age four.

2 EARLY LEARNING

The School of Hard Knocks

Adam had his Fourth Birthday. There was cake and presents abound. Adam was delighted to partake of cakes and other goodies shaped like his favorite Icons of the early nineteen-nineties. To some of whom lack an understanding of the human culture, it might look somewhat barbaric to eat pictures of what one loved, but this is commonplace in our modern age and is seldom given much thought.

After enjoying a delicious cake, Adam decided to play with some other human children. It should be noted that there were no other cat hybrid families around. Thankfully they were able to blend in by hiding their cattails within their pants. Their ears were the same color as their heads. Their excuse for appearing to not have ears was that it was a birth defect, but they could still hear without them. Because Californians value vanity, they wore prosthetic human ears. Additionally, they were the only known Jewish family on the block. Regardless it didn't seem to bother anyone from what he could tell. Adam enjoyed the company of others and was probably one of the happiest kids anyone would ever meet.

Neighbors of interest at this point in time included the "Major" family. The "Major" family consisted of Steve, Heidi, Sarah, and Scott. The Major Family lived in the house to the left of Adams and had a pool built in their backyard. Moreover, their home was two stories tall, just like Adam's. The neighbors to the right of Adam's house were the "Brown" Family. The "Brown" family consisted of Guy, Maria, and Nicky. They were one of the only two African American households in the neighborhood.

After a happy birthday celebration complete with presents and toys, it was decided Adam would be enrolled in a preschool to nurture social skills and early learning. Adam's days from that point on were fun and carefree.

As far as he knew, friends seemed to come and go, and when he asked, his mom would usually say, "I got mad at their mother." Adam only had friends because his mom was friends with their mom. He kept to himself otherwise and was pretty independent when it came to playtime. This lifestyle could not last for long. One morning his mother and father left for work. Adam didn't want to go to preschool that day.

Adam had no way of knowing the irresistible opportunity his decision presented to Tara and Cara. Weeks ago, his curiosity got the better of him, and worse still, the sisters were developing hormones that made them irrational at times and overall hard to be around. Adam went downstairs to eat breakfast. After eating breakfast, Adam headed upstairs to play with his toys in his room but was stopped.

Tara was the first to speak. "Where do you think you are going?"

Adam replied, "I am going to my room, and I will play with my toys."

Tara replied, "Not right now, you won't, we have some unfinished business to take care of here."

Cara and Tara approached Adam with their fists, ready to beat him up.

Adam asked, "What did I do?"

Adam cried out, "Please don't hurt me!"

Adam was cornered punches were thrown by Cara and Tara, and although they left no noticeable bruises, they still hurt. Adam had never been in one of those violent situations before and didn't know what to do. They continued to beat his body with their punches and kicks even when he was lying on the ground. Adam screamed for mom in pain.

Tara and Cara said in unison in a taunting voice, "Mom's not here!"

Adam was in tears and in pain. The amount of time it went on for remains unknown. To Adam, it felt like they'd done so all day and enjoyed the sound of his screams and cries of pain and sorrow. By the time his parents returned home, it was all over, and Adam hugged them in tears, the sisters had gone back to their room. Joanne and David assumed Adam had missed them. Adam didn't know how to tell them what had gone on and could not understand long term consequences.

In other words, if an action didn't happen the instant, he did something wrong or was wronged, he couldn't make the connections of cause and effect. Therefore, if they had decided on any punishments later, it was his belief they got off scot-free. From that day on, he never wanted to stay home from preschool again if he had the choice.

When Adam was in preschool, songs were sung before meals to teach self-control. If he could wait till all the nonsense was done, he'd be allowed to have seconds for snacks and meals, if he desired.

If he was too hungry to wait for the singing to end, he only got one helping. All children in the preschool wore name tags that were put on the shirts of the children each day they were there.

On Tuesday, it was music day. On music day, a child got a sticker every time they answered a question correctly. For example, "What instrument is this?" Children were not expected to just know what the answer is, so the instructor would pull out instruments name them, ask the class to repeat the name, shuffle them, and then ask the question. In other words, it was more a test of their visual and auditory memory. If a child answered it correctly, they got a sticker to put on their nametag. Adam had always raised his hand to answer the questions. Never in his entire year at the preschool did he get a single question wrong. Adam would always come home on Tuesdays with a nametag littered in stickers, and his parents never knew why. They smiled supportively as he showed them off nonetheless. As fun as the preschool was, Adam met his first bully there too, his name was Paul.

Paul, for whatever reason, seemed to enjoy punching people in the classroom even if his punches weren't enough to knock anyone over, they did sting. Adam would always tell on him, but the worst Paul got was a scolding. In fact, he was the only one in the preschool who got a pillow during naptime. Adam came to a conclusion. Hitting is ok if you are angry even if people do not like it. He would soon learn that notion doesn't apply to everyone.

Like any good scientist, Adam explored that hypothesis and got sent to the office for hitting a kid who made him angry. Adam's conclusion was, "Anger is bad, and one must not get angry unless they want to get in trouble." Music and snacks were not the only things Adam enjoyed.

He would sometimes play on swings or other playground equipment. Other days he'd lay on a bench and pretend to sleep while in actuality be staring into the clouds reflecting on life and pondering his purpose in it. Sometimes his efforts alone would be fruitless.

When that happened, he would enjoy asking adults that would talk to him, questions about why things happen. He would later call these discussions of life to people older than him, "Socratic dialogs."

Adam didn't understand the purpose of socializing. He did, however, find it an enjoyable way to share knowledge and get different perspectives on life. In kindergarten, he would learn that not everyone his age shared his sensibilities.

3 KINDERGARTEN

The School of Softer Knocks

The next year Adam had entered Kindergarten in the fall because his Birthday was in the summer. In America, Public Education doesn't start until one is almost five years old and can be earlier or later, depending on one's season of birth, among other things. The name of the school was "Cypresses Clothes Are Fashionable Elementary." Adam, unlike other kids, seemed happy to be starting school and furthering his understanding of the world. He was pleased to meet the teacher and talk with her when she was not in a lecture. His kindergarten teacher's name was "Ms. Vaguely." Ms. Vaguely was impressed by Adam's love of gaining knowledge by any means necessary. Adam was also learning how to play the SNES. Tara owned the SNES, and Adam was fascinated by some of the games.

Sometimes he would even talk to Ms. Vaguely about the various video games he played. She was a kind-hearted person and tried to be fair with people while doing her job as a teacher. Overall, she did it well. Adam was at recess, watching some of the kids play.

The boys were yelling, "No girls Allowed!" on the playground near a tunnel.

At this point in life, Adam was unaware of "genders" and didn't understand why the other boys were so threatened by these "girls."

Ms. Vaguely stepped in and said, "How about no boys allowed?"

Her words were met with an awkward silence. Adam wasn't sure what to make of all this.

One day, a teacher's aide Ms. Millais noticed Adam sitting on the sidelines, watching everything happen. Adam's absent answers as to why conflicts occurred saw it as a time to learn by observation or think about life. Ms. Millais asked him why he wasn't playing with the other kids.

"Play with the other children?"

"They are mean to each other, and most of them barely know how to blow their nose.

"What is this 'playing with others' you speak of?"

It was explained to him, and he was reassured all would be ok, it was, and Adam was content to play with whoever as gender was a foreign concept to him. However, there was one day, when he was playing with a toy phone with a girl that he realized how little he knew of communicating with people his age. He just copied words he'd heard his dad use which unknown to him were words that his peers wouldn't know until they were in fourth grade at least. The responses of the children were that of silence and puzzled stares.

Besides recess, other class activities included bringing a toy from home on a particular day. The day of the week would always be the same and who brought one and when would depend on the first letter of one's name. Additionally, each participant would have about five to fifteen minutes for the class to guess what he or she brought to school-based only on the first letter of the object's name.

In other words, if one brought a teddy bear, one would say it began with a "t," and the class would spend about five to fifteen minutes trying to guess what it was. There was no prize for guessing correctly, nor was there a penalty if no one could guess what it was. As a student, Adam preferred to sit as close to the teacher as possible. It turned out he wasn't the only one who did either, and this would cause arguments over who got to sit in front of the teacher. This was when he made his first school enemy. Her name was Elisabeth, but everyone called her Liz.

She would sometimes lightly hit him when the teacher was reading or push him out of his square spot on the carpet when the teacher was lecturing. They didn't have desks in the reading room and spent their days sitting on the carpet inside of tape lines that formed square shapes. Occasionally a student would be called out of class to work on writing letters with the teacher's aide later on in the semester; they did basic addition math or pre arithmetic skills. All in all, Adam enjoyed Kindergarten and celebrated any non-Christian holidays. He was a bumblebee for Halloween that year. Things were mostly good for Adam until first grade.

4 FIRST GRADE

The Traditional Teacher from Hell

The first day of a brand-new school year had begun. Adam was six years old or close to it and had taken on a different personality. Once Adam finally knew he was a boy, it was the desire of his to be a metaphorical modern-day chivalrous knight. On the playground, whether it was his job on the job rotation board in the class or not, he enjoyed escorting people to the nurse's office, especially females. For some reason doing so always gave him a warm fuzzy feeling inside.

In the classroom was another story entirely. His teacher, "Ms. Young," had demands Adam had never imagined. Unlike Ms. Vaguely, she didn't enjoy talking to him, and she was far more demanding of him. Projects consisted of occasional in-class readings, writing, spelling, and arithmetic. He was also told to do art projects and the like regularly. It was in this classroom that he learned a new lesson. "Time is not your friend anymore." She only gave students fifteen minutes or less to do a single writing assignment spelling task or art project, and then it was on to the next thing.

Adam was good at speech-based activities, but due to dexterity issues, he had trouble putting his ideas on paper. It was expected after time that he would have to write and spell words in cursive, but like many people today would say, "I can't believe I was made to learn that useless skill." The difference is he never learned it. His spelling tests would turn up "F's" not because he couldn't spell. In fact, he was above average at it. He just couldn't write it. Ms. Young would often yell at him in front of the class for his incompetence when it came to writing. He felt like a total idiot, and this slowly got to him. Adam was Angered by this blatant disregard for the fact that he was trying his best to make the grade. Due to disorders not well known at the time, let alone accommodated, he earned a new title, "The

Trouble Maker." He would do everything the teacher told him not to do when he felt she was rude to him about his academic difficulties. Since resorting to physical violence would have gotten him into worse trouble, it was the next best thing.

Despite his antics, he managed to make some friends and had typical friendships where visitations to home, birthday parties, and other fun things happened. Some of his closest friends were Bonnie, Melissa, Jennifer, Jermaine, Joshua, and Leticia.

Jermaine and Joshua were Asian neighbors, the only ones in his neighborhood who were. Adam never found out which Asian country their family line was from. Bonnie was a Taiwanese girl, Melissa was white with blond hair, Jennifer was white with brown hair. He questioned his friendship with Jennifer because she was usually mean to him unless he had goodies around. Leticia, his first African American friend, was the most unlikely friend because Adam's first reaction to meeting her may have been misinterpreted to be racist. He'd never seen Guy or Maria or Nicky then, or anyone in the person of that, and the only African Americans he'd ever seen were on TV. He was told most likely by Tara that everything on it was not real. So, one can only imagine the awkwardness of meeting someone of another race then. Luckily, she was cool with it, and they became pretty tight, all things considered.

Adam spent some time trying to be friends with Jennifer. He saw she enjoyed doing flips on monkey bars. This sometimes leads to her getting hurt and wanted to make sure to help her at a moment's notice. Other kids in the school who he didn't know had spread a rumor about him "liking" Jennifer. Adam didn't understand what people meant when they asked if he "liked" Jennifer. He thought they were talking about liking as friends, but he was sorely mistaken. Misunderstandings of the like caused situations to escalate to the point of bullying. Adam was often teased by the other guys. Adam didn't let it get to him and tried to avoid playing with others on the playground ever since.

As weeks went on, his mom and dad would have their date nights and leave Cara and Tara in charge of him. This was a big mistake. Tara and Cara capitalized on Adam's fear of them from when he was four years old. Tara enjoyed playing video games often and never let Adam play unless the parents demanded it of her, and Cara, who was content to just watch, made Adam, their slave. Adam was supposed to toast waffles for them or fetch things they asked for. He also learned to cook through such enslavement.

By the time he finished serving them, he had almost zero energy to do anything else. So, if he wanted waffles, he ate them raw with butter and syrup once they defrosted enough. He can still recall feelings of emptiness and sorrow and fear all at the same time through enslavement. Sometimes Tara would cook for him, but only if he managed not to tick her off more than Cara.

To put it simply, if he managed not to piss her off for the week, he would have large quantities of food. Otherwise, he would be on his own to make dinner. Joanne would, on rare occasions, catch Tara hitting him, but the worst she got was yelled at by mom from what one could tell. If he retaliated even if, in self-defense, he immediately got a time out.

From these combined experiences, he learned another lesson. "Apparently, it is ok to be hit but not ok to defend yourself." It was at that point that he realized if he tattled on them, it wouldn't do him any good. In his mind, everyone saw him as the troubled child while Tara was the "genius" of the family who maybe had a few anger issues sometimes.

Adam tried everything he could think of to be the apple of his parent's eyes. He would happily lay out silverware on the dinner table when the parents were home and happy to hear a thank you for his efforts. Tara always seemed angry in response to Adam's acts of goodwill for the family.

Despite the fact he wasn't wholly hated, he knew he couldn't unleash his anger at home nor at school. Additionally, using words to people who picked on him was useless at venting anger unless he used profanity. Realizing people got offended by a child using strong language and didn't like him hitting people even if it was in self-defense; He slowly became a ticking time bomb waiting to go off with minimal stimulus.

This was part of the reason why Adam avoided playing with other kids because he knew that if they won a game against him or if he interacted with them, there was a chance he'd get angry. When angered, he would try to run away. If that didn't work, he'd vent his anger by swearing like a sailor. This would result in them go give their signature you're in trouble sound. His only other option was to physically attack them. Running away wouldn't work in school because this would either require him to go off campus or leave the playground, which was not permitted unless he was escorting someone who was hurt, doing a favor for a teacher, or got hurt and had to see a nurse. The best he could hope for was not being forced to interact with other kids at all. This worked for a good portion of the semester. Then came a day when, despite trying to explain his dislike of competition and what he was afraid would happen if it got too out of hand to a recess lady responded by making an ultimatum.

"Play with the other kids or be given a 'pink slip."

For those that are unfamiliar with a pink slip in elementary school, it meant one would be reported to their classroom teacher for further disciplinary action. Basically, a pink slip was what most schools call an office or classroom referral. Too many acts of "defiance" would result in being sent to the principal's office. Knowing this, Adam saw no way out.

He gave in to her demands and said, "Fine, but if I get angry, and the situation gets inappropriate or out of hand, don't say I didn't warn you."

Adam reluctantly played with the other kids, and it was just as he feared, and worst of all, he got the pink slip anyway, and an unsympathetic Ms. Young was waiting for him in the classroom.

She said, "Get in trouble out there, and you get in trouble here. Now, go change your card!"

Ms. Young had a card system set up to control her class. If one stayed on the "green" card, one got a sticker at the end of the day. If one managed to get a certain number of them which would have taken the entire school year to accumulate, especially for one like Adam impossible, one would get a plush of one's choice from her collection of teddy bears.

In fact, if Adam even pretended to hum, he'd have to go up there to change it. Followed by, it was a "yellow" card, which meant no sticker at the end of the day, and nothing else happened. The "blue" card was next, and one was sent to detention. "orange" card meant not only the penalties of the previous cards but a note home to parents. The last card was a "black" card, and if one went that far, they were sent to the principal's office.

It was safe to say that Adam spent many days in detention and had many notes sent home. Worse still, even when he tried to be good and get his work done, he was forced to attend Saturday school because of his sloppy but improving penmanship. Only when he was allowed to print by hand rather than write in cursive did he show any progress.

If that wasn't bad enough when December came around, Ms. Young ordered him to participate in singing Christmas songs despite him being Jewish. The only thing good that she did for him at that time was to let his mom introduce the class to Hanukkah and make Hanukkah decorations. Otherwise, he got no special exemption for conflicting religious beliefs to not sing in it. Adam didn't mind listening to it as he'd grown used to it being the thing all kids were expected to do, but to sing them was akin to being converted to Christianity in his mind or blasphemy to his own upbringing. When given an ultimatum of being sent to the principal's office, he sang reluctantly and didn't bother telling his parents about the threat.

When Christmas and Hanukkah came, his grandma grandpa and great-grandma came to visit. His grandma was so mean; she would spank him for flipping a cat's ears. Grandpa was ok and often took his share of insanity from Grandma. Great Grandma would sit by herself much like Adam used to at school, and this intrigued him.

He approached her and said, "I couldn't hurt you."

"And I couldn't spank you," she replied.

Adam smiled and began talking to her for a while, asking many existential questions about things that happen in life and why they do. He was happy to learn she was well-read and a deep thinker. Adam had finally found someone that understood him. He enjoyed playing with her, and she found a way to take the competitive feel out of any game and get Adam so lost in conversation he'd forget he was even playing a game.

Hanukkah was pretty standard for him. Eight nights of gifts, menorah lighting, and prayers and wouldn't change much from one year to the next save the presents he got. He didn't like the taste of Latkes, but he did enjoy playing the "dreidel" game with his family for chocolate gelt.

He loved the taste of the chocolates more than most, and since he had a lot of it that year, he wanted to share the joy of them, so he slipped a few chocolate coins between the crevices of the gifts his parents made for friends and neighbors when no one was looking. It made no difference to him whether the items were for Hanukkah or Christmas.

He was told the story of how if not for a Menorah staying lit for eight days and eight nights while the Israelites went to get more oil for their oil lamps because they didn't have electricity or light bulbs back then there would be no Hanukkah. The Dreidel game was explained to be a loophole in laws that forbid Jews from practicing Judaism under the rule of King Antiochus. Judah Maccabee was the one to lead the resistance to reclaim Judea and ultimately won. Adam figured it a much better story than one of a fat guy coming down your chimney and giving you gifts only if you were well behaved that year and believed blindly in him. Hanukkah was probably the only time in December when Cara and Tara weren't cruel to him; thus, he looked forward to it every year. The rest of December and the year was fair game to them. At the end of the holiday season, each grandparent gave him and the siblings twenty dollars from each of them. Adam had sixty dollars to spend that year and subsequent ones at that time of year. The monetary gift was matched to all family members on their respective birthdays. Adam knew he would miss the connection he'd made with his great-grandma when she had to go back to Michigan and promised to send letters often.

Basically, his grandparents weren't within driving distance of him unless he took a week-long road trip or longer before he even reached them, let alone got to spend even a day with them. It became a hobby for him throughout the rest of the school year. He also exchanged stickers with her by mail as a hobby.

When his First elementary year came to a close, Adam was happy. He and his classmates would be the last ones to ever have to deal with Ms. Young at that school. Ms. Young said that she was moving to Boston. In the end, the entire class got to pick out a teddy bear anyway because no one could meet her standards when it came to behavior except one or two, and they got to pick two of them. Adam picked out one that was big but had slanted eyes. One of the other kids said that it was blind, and Adam told them that he didn't care.

5 SECOND GRADE AND LITTLE LEAGUE BASEBALL

The Number Loving Teacher and the Crazy Mom

Adam finally got a half-decent teacher who was kind again, her name was Ms. Sutton. She was very enthusiastic about everything she taught, even math. In fact, one time, Adam came in, and she told him to do a chant that went, "Two, four, six, eight who do we appreciate even numbers!" Adam just sort of mouthed it because after the teacher he had the previous year, he wasn't as enthusiastic about education anymore least of all math, which often caused him to doze off in class. This would not do, and eventually, he caved in and said it half-heartedly. As far as other school things, not much had changed.

During this time, Adam played little league baseball and brought home participation trophies. He wasn't the best in it, but there were worse players. His mom Joanne, however, was not faring so well during this time. There was one time at a Shake-Me-Like-a-Rattle's Pizza, where his mom completely flipped her lid. The baseball team Adam played for was given two pepperoni pizzas. No one was vegetarian, and no one knew anything about Jewish people or their dietary laws.

This caused Joanne to have an episode. She grabbed Adam's hand and walked him around the pizza parlor.

"They are feeding him pork! They are feeding him pork!"

Eventually, she came to her senses and let Adam go back to the table with his team. One of Adam's coaches asked what it was all about.

Adam shrugged and said, "I don't know something about feeding me pork."

"We aren't feeding you, pork."

Adam plucked the pepperonis off his pizza and ate the pizza leaving them behind. As weeks and months went on, it wasn't uncommon for him to listen to messages on the home phone to find one from mom or dad saying that mom was taken to charter oak hospital and would be away for at least a week. This happened seven times between then and when he turned nine.

Due to the medicines, she took for Clinical Depression, she could sleep for at least eighteen hours straight before needing to eat.

This resulted in Adam not being able to go to many social events.

When he'd try to wake her up for them, she'd say "I'm not sleeping, I am resting."

Adam would usually reply, "You've been doing that for over twelve hours."

Adam really missed his mom when she was in the mental hospital and when she was tranquilized. Adam had no idea how messed up she was.

6 ADAM THE SAD STRANGE LITTLE MAN

The Smart Alek Third Grader Learns His Place Again

In summer, Adam had to attend summer school at Ben Lomond Elementary School when he met Christina, who was interestingly enough was the daughter of one of Adam's summer school teachers. It happened to be the teacher who taught computer skills to people of his grade.

The Teacher would be the one Adam had first thing in the morning, and her name was "Heidi Clauss." Her daughter, "Christina," had the same last name as her mother. Christina Clauss was five and a half, and Adam was almost eight years old at the time. He sat in front of her in class and was simply enamored with her. After his first class with her in it, the two exchanged contact information and quickly became friends.

Adam thought about her a lot from then on and would sometimes draw pictures of her and him playing together regardless of how poorly drawn they were. In some other classes, he would work together with her. As time went on, Adam learned she was very high in the reading level and other skills as well. Adam finally felt understood intellectually and had someone who could demonstrate it admirably on paper. They were a perfect match, or so he thought. That fall, Adam returned to "Cypresses Clothes Are Fashionable."

Though the summer was mostly pleasant, he developed a defensive A-list mentality.

He was told by a teacher Ms. Holstein, "You write like a first grader!"

"I know I came to school, hoping I could learn how to write better," Adam replied.

Adam either didn't know or didn't care that his words were pretty much saying, "I know, so why aren't you teaching me.

He was tired of being ridiculed or scolded for his academic

shortcomings and tired of being a slave or punching bag to his sisters. Adam found it odd

that not long after his snarky remark, Cara had utterly lost her mind and wouldn't take her medication. Not being the bad guy for a change felt great, and Adam sadistically enjoyed watching her act out. It was after they took her to the mental hospital and threatened to make her stay there that Adam got a brilliant plan on how to escape his troubles even if only temporarily.

He feigned insanity and was just as destructive as Cara was weeks later when he'd simply had enough of life. When he was taken there, he asked if the food was any good to his mom, who told him it wasn't bad. With her seal of approval, Adam agreed to stay there. The sad part is except for the entry blood test, everything was better there for him than at home. He learned to live with a roommate, and all was good until the last two nights.

He kept a glow in the dark teddy bear to help him cope through life that he'd had since he was a baby. One day he had the bossiest most sociopathic roommate he'd ever known. The roommate was so messed up that the moment Adam was put in a room with him, the roommate gave Adam a long list of "don'ts," and "if you, dos." The one that struck him hardest was the threat to tear his precious teddy bear to shreds. So for the rest of that night before his release day, he couldn't sleep a wink and toss and turned like crazy. The sociopath was trusted by the staff to call them whenever Adam did something. Then on release day, Adam was playing checkers by himself on a paper checkerboard as usual.

It was then that a fat blond-haired girl who appeared to be about fifteen and always called him, "A sad, strange little man" or just, "little man," approached him. She knocked his checkerboard off the table on purpose.

Adam responded by yelling, "Hey, pick that up, you slob!"

Her response was to call in the entire unit of at least eleven and a maximum of twenty-two teenagers to beat him up as they threw their punches. He made pain sounds and uttered the "S" word with each one. When he finally hit the floor, they scrammed, leaving him for dead. He was walloped, and the wind was knocked out of him, something that had never happened before.

A Staff member who was a male came out and asked Adam if he was ok.

He replied weakly, barely able to breathe enough to say anything said slowly and between labored breaths, "They must be punished!"

He then buried his face into his arms on the ground to hide the tears he was crying.

The staff member responded by saying, "Well... you are going home today.

"Come in when you are ready."

Adam lay there for about five to ten minutes before picking himself up, still sniffling a little from the ordeal, and ran to his room for the remainder of his stay. Because Adam was pretty used to this kind of treatment back home, he didn't bother to tell his parents because he'd never known them to do anything in the past to stop this even if they saw a portion of it.

Adam was happy to return back to his mostly healthy life. Everything was, for the most part, better until he randomly recounted a memory to a random boy. The story got twisted entirely around, and he was told on for something that never happened.

Somehow, "When I was little and thought I was the family pet, I drank from the dog's water dish," turned into "I drank from the toilet."

Adam showed up at the Principal Browns' office, where he was being lectured on how unsanitary his supposed acts were and didn't spend a single second listening to Adam's side of the story but demanded he continues to listen. "Principal Brown" is not the same as "Guy Brown, the neighbor." He is white and has no familial relation to them. Eventually, Adam had enough.

"Alright, if you aren't going to listen to anything, I say with regards to my innocence, then I demand that you reveal my prosecutor!

"I know my rights! I will make certain he never lies to you again!"

After that last thing, Adam said, the Principal stopped lecturing and began typing something on the computer explaining that Adam would have to find another Elementary school and that the offense for which Adam was accused would go on his permanent record. He most likely told Adam's parents a slightly different version of what had happened as administrators tend not to speak the whole truth if the parents know the law. Adam's parents knew the law and weren't afraid to show it in the past

.

7 LARK GO TO HELEN WAITE

Life Gets Worse

Adam went to what was supposed to be a better school for the remainder of third grade. Adam went back to his usual routines regarding the playgrounds but was trapped inside a tunnel by two other boys. Adam demanded they let him out, but they refused until recess was over, but Adam didn't know their names, so he couldn't tell on them.

In the classroom, kids made obnoxious gestures at him and other things to make him angry. In that school, the disciplinary system instead of a principal's office visit unless one was ultimately out of control and hurting people was a point sheet. A total number of points would be tallied per hour, totaling up to five points an hour. This point sheet system, contrary to the one he would soon see in Cortez People Attack U, included an "R" grade, which pretty much meant "I reminded you that you are in school and that is not ok." This was done before a point deduction each hour for each offense."

At the End of the day, the points would be tallied, and Level five was the highest one could get and typically only allowed for maybe one or two mess-ups to be point deductions. Level four and level three were where one wanted to be at a minimum. Level two and Level one was about the worst days one could have. The higher one's level was at the end of the day, the more privileges one had to choose from the next day. Long chapter short, it wasn't more than half a year before he'd end up in the one school that would finally make him snap.

At about this time, Jermaine and Joshua moved out and the house, and it was put up for rent. The family renting it was a white family that had a child named "Daniel" who had a physical disability whereby his bones were fragile. Adam used to try to play with him with toys he had got from a place called "Club Disney," which was unknown to him on its way out of business. Unfortunately, Daniel didn't know how to play nice with the toys and ended up breaking a Toy story Buzz Light year Toy he'd gotten for a previous birthday. Adam was angry, but since the toy still worked and the only damage to the toy was a broken space helmet, he let it go.

8 CORTEZ PEOPLE ATTACK U! (PAU)

Has a Nicer Ring to it than Hell on Earth

Adam was sent to a school for the mentally disturbed and spent a decent year for the most part except for one thing. Just getting to the school meant the high school kids and middle school kids who attended the same campus as the elementary school kids would make a game of pounding him on the head or in the gut every time the bus would stop just getting to school. Almost all of the kids that went to that school consisted of racial or religious minorities, and more than half of them were more messed up than Adam. They all had disorders far more Severe than Asperger's or ADHD, which were what he was diagnosed with when he entered that school. In previous years, his Psychiatrist was reluctant to place a single diagnosis on him but prescribed pills for him anyway for ADHD and Depression.

His mom, by that point, was doing better with her depression, having found the right pill balance, and his sister Cara had been found to have Epilepsy and Mild Retardation. Tara and David were the only ones undiagnosed in his immediate family. If that wasn't bad enough, the constant people losing their grip on their sanity throughout the school made it difficult for Adam to concentrate.

Adam's Teacher was "Mike Gonzales" and the two staff consisting of a Central American named "Kiana" and a white older staff member named "Rita." Sometimes he would be doing his work in class, looking up definitions for things, and find other intriguing words. When it was found out, he was doing this. Kiana and Mike made no hesitation in giving him grief for taking too long to do the work to which

Adam replied, "Well, I am sorry I took the extra time to actually learn something. I thought that is what school was for, but I guess I was wrong."

By now, the reader could probably guess that this ticked them off immensely, and he was perhaps subject to disciplinary action laughing through it all. Cortez People Attack U Also used almost the same point sheet system as Lark Go to Helen Waite, except their scoring criteria left no room for reminder letters on it before deducting points. Likewise, he would earn a maximum of three points for getting the work done and two points for good behavior per hour.

If he were sleeping, he'd still earn the behavior points for the hour but not the work ones. Needless to say, Adam was willing to put up with moments like that as long as he still had contact with his friends. Once word spread, he went to that "mental school" He stopped getting answers when he called people the last of which was his childhood crush "Christina."

His last words to her on her answering machine after not getting a callback and not getting an answer when he tried for over three months to reach her was, "I-I love you…"

Since that time Adam let himself come to school later and later, and some days he just wouldn't come in at all because he hated it so much there and it's not like they'd have sent a truant officer when one goes to a mental school. The psychological school administrators had more pressing concerns than worrying about how awful a student's attendance record was or whether or not their excuse was valid. If a student didn't come, it was a relief to them as it was one less unstable person they'd have to deal with. The staff did, however, yell at Adam when he'd come in late doubly so if he also notified them in advance of future absences to come.

Both Adam and the people who worked at the school knew he barely belonged there if he did at all and didn't want to be there, so Adam couldn't fathom why they would care if he didn't show up and got behind in his work or came in late. It wasn't as though most people cared half the time about learning anything. Most of the people who bullied him didn't have a mom or dad, and if they did, their moms and dads were abusive to them or uncaring. Spoiler alert, they would be put out of their misery soon enough.

If that wasn't demoralizing enough, Daniel, the fragile neighbor, moved out and was replaced by the most stereotypical group of African American teenagers he would ever meet. Not only that, but they were Anti-Semitic. Adam tried his best to represent his people. Adam never asked their names because Adam was so interested in playing with them that it didn't even cross his mind.

Adam mentioned his Jewish roots while playing basketball with them. They were significantly better at making baskets than him.

When the game ended, they said: "Jews Can't Play Basketball."

Adam bluffed that he'd be coming back with his own basketball, and thus he never came back to their place.

After all of this, Adam learned that no amount of material possessions can fill the void of friends. He also learned that those same possessions he cherished throughout his life could not quell his vindictive spirit. It was because of those realizations he swore that sooner or later, he had to get out of that hellhole school. When winter came around, Adam made plans to run away from home. His life was about to change indeed but not quite in the way he had expected.

9 THE FINAL SOLUTION

The Unspeakable Evil

It was just one more day until the Christmas Party would be held at every school Adam ever attended. Adam packed a bag of nonperishables to get himself by and his glow in the dark teddy bear. He then headed for the Covina Library.

Adam said in a low tone when no one was in earshot,

"Someday, the people here will pay for their transgressions.

"If these 'good Christians' or 'good citizens' in the larger society think it righteous to send racial and religious minorities to a mental school for being a victim their entire lives, then I want nothing to do with them.

"I must find a place where I belong. Surely someone out there can help me.

"Until then, I'd best not venture out into the world without a few survival guidebooks.".

Adam finally reached the library and went to the section of the library called "The Book Nook" where the library sold some of its books. It was there that Adam's life would never be the same again. He found a black book written in Hebrew letters.

Despite being Jewish, Adam was never taught Hebrew, and he did not attend a place of worship for Jewish people in the area. He asked the salesperson how much she wanted for it.

She said: "Just take it. No one else wants it."

Adam took the book and asked a librarian to translate the title for him.

The librarian read it and said, "Book of Necromancy Do not Open."

Adam looked at her, puzzled.

The Librarian replied, "I wouldn't worry about it. The person who gave it to us seemed pretty crazy and superstitious, so it's probably nothing."

Adam took back the book and went outside to read it out of curiosity or at least see what would happen if he opened it.

When he opened the book, screams of ghosts and demonic spirits were heard. If anyone were watching this happen, it would look like the ghosts and demonic spirits entered Adam's body and head. Adam felt a massive rush of dark power he'd never felt before. If that wasn't strange enough, he could now read the book. It had in the process of releasing the spirits attuned to it, transliterated itself phonetically so one could pronounce the spells inside it. The words were also translated into English so he'd know what they did.

With an evil grin on his face, he said to himself, "Perfect! No longer must I suffer at the hands of the human race or my sisters!"

Possessed by this new power and lust for revenge for all the transgressions of the human race and his sisters, he headed home to initiate his master plan. It was a group therapy night for his mom, so she was not back when he got there. His dad was still at work, and his sisters had just come home from school. Tara Scowled at him, sensing something was very wrong.

"Wipe that stupid smile off your face before I do it for you!" she said.

He stopped smiling and quietly mumbled a spell to summon some undead in the backyard.

Tara went to the backyard door to see for herself what was happening. She was frozen with fear hoping they wouldn't notice her. Adam took that opportunity to go upstairs to his sisters' room, where Cara was sitting by herself coloring in a book.

"Adam, what are you doing in our room?" Cara asked.

Adam replied, "Something I should have done a long time ago.

"Do you remember the time you and Tara beat me up when I was maybe four, and you guys were thirteen?

"No matter how loud I screamed in agony for mom, your response and hers was 'Mom's Not Here!'

"Well, whether you do or not, I am here to get payback for that day and for every day that I was made to suffer because of your unforgivable actions and Tara's."

Cara covered her head in fear expecting Adam to hit her there. She was wrong. Adam punched her in the stomach, causing the wind to be knocked out of her.

"Adam… P-please stop. I am sorry for everything really!" she slowly uttered barely able to breathe correctly, let alone talk.

"I am sorry, but you shouldn't have joined in with Tara in making my life a living hell.

"You could have stayed out of it, and we would not be in this situation right now.

"You did not, and now you are going to die!" Adam said in a cold and indifferent voice.

He then extended his nails being a cat hybrid; it was something he could have done but never occurred to him until now to do. Then Adam shoved a toy into her mouth to muffle her screams so Tara couldn't hear her. Cara tried to scream for mom.

Adam replied, "Mom's Not Here!" in the same taunting tone as he remembered his sisters using when they beat him up.

With that, his paw jabbed straight into her chest and ripped out her heart. Adam put it into a bathroom sink and dragged her body to the bathtub in the sisters' bedroom and then ran some water, which he put on a towel to wipe up any traces of blood. Once he had cleaned as well as he could, he carried the heart hastily downstairs to the kitchen and put it into the blender to make it into a drink.

Tara was screaming at the zombies outside, who was getting closer to the backyard door. There was a bat in her hands, and she was ready to smash their heads in. Once the heart was thoroughly blended, he mixed it with some Kool-Aid and Gatorade and poured it into a cup for Tara. The Kool-Aid and Gatorade masked the smell of blood and organ fluids. Adam chanted a spell to dismiss his zombies for now.

Tara came into the kitchen and yelled: "What were zombies doing outside our door?"

Adam replied, "I have no idea, but I figured if these were our last days on earth as mortals, I might as well make a drink for you as a final act of kindness."

Tara said, "you always were a kiss ass, and I resented it, but thanks."

She chugged it down because she was dehydrated from screaming. It left a bad taste in her mouth.

"Yuck! What is this nasty stuff?

"Didn't I teach you to serve better food and drink than this?" she asked.

"To answer your second question, yes, you did, and to answer your first, let's just say I haven't the heart to tell you!" Adam answered.

Tara thought for a moment what Adam could have meant by that, and her eyes went wide.

"No way…you didn't!" she yelled.

Adam smiled, "Well, you could check upstairs after all she could have just had constipation on the toilet or something."

Tara hoped this was all a sick joke and followed his advice to check on Cara. Tara found Cara's body and screamed loud enough to shake the house. While in shock, his next-door neighbor, "Maria," was calling nine-one-one. Adam got to work severing the landlines at home. When he was done, he called back the zombies, one of which saw Maria dialing nine-one-one with an expression of panic on her face when he opened the backyard door to let the zombies inside.

Tara regained her composure and ran to the landline in the parents' room to try and call nine-one-one to find the lines were cut, and no one in the family-owned a cellphone at the time. Tara swore profusely and ran downstairs, hoping to make a break for the front door only to find Adam was waiting for her.

"Going somewhere, Tara?" He asked while some zombies stood behind him, awaiting his commands.

Tara replied, "You! You did this, didn't you?"

Adam laughed evilly.

"That's right! But you aren't going anywhere, Tara I hated you most of all!

"Also, that drink was Cara's heart." He said in a sociopathic voice devoid of any remorse, sorrow, or regret.

Tara was furious that Adam would kill one of his own flesh and blood and feed it to another. Tara had seen enough horror movies to know that even if she ran, Adam would catch up to her sooner or later. From best Tara figured, the best option was to try and kill him here and now. Tara lunged at Adam in an attempt to take him to the ground. Adam sidestepped to her left, causing Tara to lose her balance and trip into the crowd of zombies. The zombies began tearing through Tara's flesh with their claws and eating her.

Adam heard police sirens outside the door.

"Come out with your hands up whoever you are!" he heard them shout through a police megaphone.

"Oh, boo! It seems the fuzz has come to crash our party!" Adam said. Using a spell from the book, Adam sent what remained of Cara and Tara to the center of the earth. Their bodies would never be found again.

Adam flipped through his spellbook and found a spell to make a death gate portal he could use to escape the house. He quickly cast it and got out of there just as police rammed the door down. The death gate disappeared once Adam entered it and found himself at a graveyard where he plotted his next move.

10 REVENGE IS A DISH BEST SERVED COLD

The Chaos Must Go On

Adam thought to himself: perfect now that I am here, I can assess the situation at hand. The cops and forensics teams will be searching the house for a while. My next targets are Cypresses Clothing Are Fashionable Today, Lark Go to Helen Waite, and Cortez People Attack U. Then there is the Charter Oak Mental Hospital. If memory serves tomorrow is the school Christmas party so that would be a good time for me to attack. Every kid in school will be there then.

Adam slept in a tree that night as forensics teams had blocked Joanne and David from returning home. With nowhere else to go, the two of them were given a hotel room at government expense while this investigation was carried out.

The next morning all of the kids he went to school with had made it to their first class. That was when Adam made his move.

Adam's first target was "Cypresses Clothes Are Fashionable Today." He ordered a hoard of zombies to block all entrances and exits to the place. He summoned a pair of Giant Skeletal hands big enough to drag the entire school to the center of the earth with everyone inside. He sent a tracker undead to Boston to track down and kill Ms. Young as well. The fate of "Lark Go to Helen Waite" and "Cortez People Attack U" was no different. He took out "Lark Go to Helen Waite" second and then "Cortez People Attack U" last. Satisfied with his work, he had his zombies build for him a suitable castle on top of the former location of Cortez PAU. He filled the castle with traps. The traps and the castle's design much resembled that of Fiend Lord Magus' castle from Chrono Trigger. Adam went inside his lair and began gathering weapons to take with him to use against the mental hospital inmates and the ones who called nine-one-one on him.

Forensic teams were still searching Adam's family home when Police, Swat Teams, and Private Investigators were called to investigate the former sites of Cypress Clothes Are Fashionable, Lark Go to Helen Waite and Cortez People Attack U.

Adam made a proper uniform for himself once he was inside his new lair. His uniform consisted of cargo shorts, no shirt, no shoes, and two tail holes in the cargo shorts for his two zebra-striped tails, and he untied his cat ears and removed the fake human ones. Last but not least, he sewed a grim reaper cloak. With the new uniform made, Adam inserted his serial killer weapons, torture devices, and a magical scythe fashioned using a spell from the book of necromancy into their slots.

The scythe can serve as both a murder weapon and a device with which to summon more powerful undead and demonic monstrosities. Besides slashing a person's head off, it can shoot darker equivalents to Sci-Fi lasers or bullets at people if desired. It is powered by both his own hatred and the hatred of the entire earth or whatever planet he happened to be on. Safe to say Adam had almost limitless ammunition available to him, considering our world has no shortage of hatred.

Once Adam had finished suiting up, he heard Sirens outside his castle. Swat Teams, Police, FBI, and PI's pulled up in front of it. This did not surprise Adam at all. In fact, it played right into his plan. He cast a spell to summon an undead clone of himself. The clone was supposed to act as a decoy so the cops would stop chasing him.

Adam opened a death gate to the home of the "Brown" family because they called nine-one-one. He knew it was them because he can see everything his undead see, so when one of his zombies saw them dialing nine-one-one while in pursuit of his sisters, he saw it too.

Once he was at the "Brown" residence, police and swat teams stormed his base after ordering to come out with his hands up. The FBI Agents and PIs followed closely behind the police and swat teams. Some were sliced into human steaks by his guillotines, and others got bombed running up one of his rooms. Still, others were devoured entirely or turned into undead by zombies in a zombie pit. The few that made it out of the hole stormed his Illusion Room, where they swore, they saw their loved ones. As they approached their loved ones, the illusions of them grew hostile and attacked them. Some were killed by them, and the others who were able to destroy what they swore were their loved ones pressed on into the next room. The survivors of the illusion room found a rope bridge over a pool of lava that had to be crossed to reach Adam's private chambers.

The decoy of Adam reappeared on the other side of the bridge and made a rude gesture and ran up the stairs behind it. As the survivors ran across the rope bridge to catch Adam, it began to spin like a hammock after one gets off of it. Despite their best efforts to hang onto the bridge, the remaining forces fell into the lava. They either lost their grip on the ropes, or they snapped under their weight.

Meanwhile, at the "Brown" residence," alarms rang nonstop. Adam didn't seem fazed at all. A nearby police station got the alarm signal on their monitors from the "Brown" house" and called in some police units from any nearby cities. Seeing as there weren't a lot of groups to take on this threat, the police called the Governor's office in Sacramento, California, and explained the situation. Governor Gray Davis called in the state troops to assist the emergency response teams.

The police knowing backup was on its way, stormed the house. Adam summoned some undead to take on the officers outside. The police opened fire on the undead, but; few of them had ever expected this to turn into a zombie battle. They were unaware of what had been causing officers to disappear, and they weren't from Michigan, so they didn't know to shoot the zombies in the head.

Inside the house, Maria and Guy came downstairs with baseball bats in their hands. Adam threw his scythe in a boomerang motion across the room, and just as they got within striking distance, they were suddenly cut in half Adam caught his weapon as it came back around. Nicky saw the entire thing and ran back to his room, closing and locking the door behind him. Adam was able to slice through it quickly with his scythe.

"You have seen too much little Nicky I won't let you tell a soul."

He ran to Nicky, who appeared to be between the ages of eight and ten years old. Adam didn't know these neighbors quite as well as he knew the "Major" Family, and even then, he didn't care.

"Do you like nursery rhymes?" Adam Asked as he pinned Nicky to the wall and removed his slipper socks.

"Well, here is one you probably already know."

He cut off Nicky's big toe and set it next to a plate of fruits and vegetables.

"This little piggy went to market!" said Adam.

Nicky screamed for mom again.

"Mom's not here! I killed her!" said Adam.

He cut off Nicky's second-largest toe and put it in a toy house.

"This little piggy stayed home!" said Adam.

Once more, Nicky screamed in agony. Adam cut off Nicky's third-largest toe and put it next to some beef in a safe oven dish and put it in the oven to be cooked.

"This little piggy had roast beef!" Adam said.

Adam cut off the second smallest toe and put it over an open fire until it burned to ash.

"This little piggy had none!" Adam said.

"And this little piggy cried 'Wee! Wee! Wee!' all the way home." said

Adam as he Cut off the smallest toe and placed it in a toy car.

After screaming at the top of his lungs throughout the removal of the last two toes, Nicky passed out from the pain.

"Aww, so peaceful sleeping like that, well, my friend only one last thing to ensure you never tell a soul."

He opened Nicky's mouth and cut his tongue out blood going everywhere. Ambulances and police vehicles could be heard outside, and the police had broken into the house.

"We'll meet again soon, little one in the hospital!" said Adam.

Adam opened a death gate out and waited at the nearest hospital, where Nicky was brought for urgent care. The police broke through the army of zombies, the state troopers behind them. They were too late to catch him. Nicky, Guy, and Maria arrived at the hospital where Adam was waiting for them. Guy and Maria had already lost too much blood to be saved, their hearts failed, and their bodies completely shut down. Nicky was patched up to stop the bleeding. The toes that were remained intact were put on ice in hopes of being reattached. Adam entered the hospital and ran into another patient's room. The patient in the room was a girl that was going to die of cancer and just finished radiation therapy.

Her bracelet read "Angie Steinburg."

"Cancer is a real pain, isn't it?

"Hmm, I would like to watch you suffer, but you are not the one I am after, and I will need a distraction to get to the one I want…" Adam said as he pulled the IV out of her arm.

The medical staff rushed to her aid. Adam ran into the operating room of the one he set out to kill. Nicky regained consciousness as Adam put on a doctor's mask, he obtained from the other hospital room.

"Hello, I will be your doctor today.

"Who ordered the liver transplant?

"Don't worry, this one is on the house!"

Using a surgeon's scalpel, he gutted open Nicky's belly, causing him to scream in agony as he pulled the IV out of Nicky's arm to deny him anesthetic. Concerned hospital staff put the IV back in Angie Steinburg's limb then ran to where Adam was operating. Adam threw needled syringes filled with tranquilizer solution at the hospital staff and locked the door after shoving them out of the room. He ripped out Nicky's liver and forced it into Nicky's mouth like an apple in a pig's mouth for roasting. Nicky's Screams were muffled as he passed out in pain and fear. Nicky's breathing stopped. Adam lit a fire and contained it in that room using a cigarette lighter that was stolen from a smoker outside and some sticks and rocks he found outside the hospital. The alarms rang loudly, and by the time the staff came to, and the police broke down the door, followed by the State Troopers who had called in any local Navy, Army, and Marine units within a 50-mile radius of Covina.

Adam was eating Nicky's liver while the rest of the body of Nicky was being roasted over the flame. Adam offered a piece of the human to one of the cops.

"Are you going to help me eat this?" He asked casually.

The police reached for their guns, as did the Marines Navy and Army units. An army of undead ambushed the underprepared units. The zombies pinned them to the ground while Adam swiftly sliced their arms off so they couldn't hold a gun with his scythe. Their actions were slower as they had never seen anything like this and were freaked out.

"Oh, goodie more souls to torture!" he said.

The zombies threw the police, Navy, Army, and Marine units into the fire. Adam listened happily as they screamed in agony and cooked alive. After eating an entire child, he was full and gave the rest of the bodies to his undead. The hospital staff tried to run away, but the exits were blocked. "I grow tired of these games. Torturing souls is such exhausting work." Adam said as he set the entire hospital on fire. Adam took a death gate out of the building as it burned and collapsed on everyone else inside. His death gate disappeared behind him, and he was back in his castle, resting. My traps will surely protect me while I sleep, he thought. Adam was exhausted from the mass killings and being on the run. He thought it best to wait until any remaining rescue workers had given up their investigations before making performing his final act of vengeance.

Weeks passed, and no matter how hard anyone searched Adam's house or the hospital that burned down. They found nothing to connect Adam to the crimes and anyone who investigated the hospital, or the three schools didn't return. There was nothing more police could do as they didn't know who was behind all this because anyone that came into contact with him never lived to tell of it. The last transmission received was that a cat boy had gone on top of the roof of the castle. With no family matching that description, it was quickly dismissed as a hoax. The hospital burning down was theorized as a problem with the gas lines within. The hospital was rebuilt. Adam was not their only problem; people tried their hardest to move on and resume life there. Rumors spread of people being taken to another realm where they could not escape the restless souls. Some people came in at night on a dare and were never seen again. As people continued to disappear without a trace, the hospital was shut down, and any remaining patients were taken to another facility.

Weeks passed, and a couple people managed to come back alive shaken by all that they had seen. Adam was watching the news to learn that he wasn't the only one killing people in the immediate area. Those he'd killed were not put to rest and were doing a lot of his work for him. The victims described scenes of friends dying just like the ghosts that appeared. That is if they had an eye cut out and other organs, the victims of the spirits would have the same happen to them. The survivors only got out thanks to the ghosts of the police and other rescue workers that died with the other victims they saw. The two survivors claimed that out of ten explorers, they were the only survivors.

The news reporter finished by saying, "The victims will receive psychiatric help at a local mental hospital."

The victims' names were not released due to the American's With Disabilities Act, which prohibits the release of medical records to the public.

Adam smiled evilly.

"Perfect! I'd nearly forgotten to kill them after what they did to me a year ago."

He went to the Charter Oak Mental Hospital, and sure enough, the same teenagers who beat him up were still there.

The staff tried to stop him, "A-Adam! We increased their sentence for what they did to you!"

"Not good enough!" Adam yelled angrily.

He summoned an army of undead. Some of the undead turned the staff into zombies. Others began ripping the flesh from the inmates as they screamed apologies to Adam. Adam found their leader from that day. She looked to be about sixteen and was fat and blond-haired.

"H-hi l-little man!" she said, shivering in fear.

"You thought I would never return?

"This little man couldn't give you the beating you deserved for what you did that day, but this one can take your pain away.

"Life must have been awful to you, and I am here to liberate you from it once and for all!"

He drew his claws and punctured her stomach ripping her intestines out to show them to her.

"I'm sorry! Please don't kill me!" she cried in pain and fear.

He licked her intestines and poured salt inside her open wounds. Her screams got louder and louder.

"Yes, scream for me your pain your agony your fear it sustains me!"

He pinned her flat on the ground as he began cutting out her eyes with his scalpel as she shrieked in pain. After he finished cutting her eyes out, she had passed out from all the blood loss and was breathing her last breaths. He cut them into little slices and squeezed their juices into a cup of lemonade laid out as the inmates were about to have a snack when he barged in. He then decorated the sides of the container with her eyeballs and began drinking it satisfied with his work. By this point, the other inmates had become fodder for his zombies. He didn't bother to clean up the mess and left a voice recording in his wake. The two who survived the other hospital tragedy were brought in. Adam was gone, and they fainted at the gristly sight. Adam left a tape recording behind. The following is the exact message on the tape recorder.

"Mortals by now, you have likely seen a lot of crazy stuff. None of you know who or what was behind all this madness.

"By the time you finish listening to this message, you will know exactly who did it. I cannot be stopped by mere mortals.

"If I am wrong and you can kill me, the ones I have killed will continue my work in my stead.

"The human race has its hands full as it is with the spirits of those I have slain as it is.

"What chance do you have against the one who is stronger even than them?

"If you are the two that survived the ghosts in the hospital, I know who you are and where you live.

"I will take my time to find you and take great pleasure in finishing you off.

"That is if the ghosts of this mental hospital don't kill you first.

"The time of the living is slowly coming to an end.

"You strive in vain as each passing day your species dies of disease, Famine, War, Homicide, Suicide, Arson, and other horrible things.

"Your kind disgusts me, and I have come to do g-d's work.

"The time for another cleansing of evil hath arrived, and I will be an angel of death!

"You may think that your fellow man is predominantly good and that your police stand up for what is right, but you are all dead wrong.

"Even among them, corruption can be found.

"In this world, many others cry out in pain and are ignored as I was.

"Where were the police when I was four years old and being beaten up by my sisters mercilessly?

"Where were the cops when at least eleven teenagers beat me up on my release day from the mental hospital?

"Where were the police when just taking the bus to get to the school for the mentally disturbed meant every time the bus stopped, one of the other riders would pound me on the head and in the gut?

"They have failed to protect me, and they have been unable to protect this world.

"I will kill everyone who comes before me out slowly and painfully, and I shall feast upon the entrails with the zombies I command.

"Bow before me and my legion, and perhaps I may let you live long enough to watch my empire rise.

"Do not even bother coming into my castle.

"My traps will make quick work of you and deny me the pleasure I crave

in gutting you myself!
"Yours Truly, Adam the Forsaken."

11 A MURDERER'S REMORSE

The Fateful Reunion

Adam the Forsaken had returned to his castle, having finished his work on Covina and West Covina. He turned on the TV to find that the recent disappearances were the first thing on the news. Police were utterly dumbfounded as any officers that called for backup claimed to see a cat person committing all these crimes, but they knew for a fact that such a thing was unlikely. Additionally, this is a world that does not believe in magic at all. So, for them to say something was dragging people to their deaths was undoubtedly dismissed as a hoax. Despite this, no one could deny that people were vanishing without a trace. Concerned citizens began packing their bags, fearing that they might be the next ones to disappear. As a result, Covina and West Covina quickly became ghost towns. Only Adam remained a resident in the areas. Adam's other next-door neighbors, the Major family had also made preparations to move out, but as Steve Major had arrived at the mental hospital to find the mess, and the tape left behind. Steve knew something was very wrong, and it hit just a little too close to home literally.

Adam was hurt by what had happened between him and the ones he thought were his friends. Despite everything that happened, Adam still loved at least one of them and knew it. Adam loved Christina, and now that he could take a death gate and go wherever he wanted, it offered him the opportunity he'd been waiting for. She would have been about eight and one-half years old by this point, if not nine years old.

Adam opened a death gate to Christina's room that night. Adam remembered when they were growing up, she used to play with him, and sometimes her annoying younger sister Cathy would come to his house, or he'd deal with her at hers. He didn't much care for Cathy at all, and as far as he knew, they shared the same bedroom, so the most significant challenge would be grabbing the one he wanted without waking the other. Adam was careful to walk slowly and quietly. Lucky for him, Christina was getting up to go to the bathroom and was sleepwalking.

Adam quietly set up a death gate in her path to the toilet after she closed the door behind her. On her way back from the bathroom, she walked right through the death gate, not even seeing it because she was asleep. Adam followed in after her. The death gate connected to Adam's room once there Christina plopped onto his bed, he went to sleep next to her cuddling her.

The following day came, and Christina woke up next to him.

She screamed, "What am I doing here? Where am I?"

Adam woke up groggily and said, "You are in my castle you were sleepwalking and ended up here.

"More importantly, did you ever get that last message I sent six months ago?"

"No," replied Christina.

Adam said, "Well, your mom probably deleted it and forbid you from seeing me."

Christina nodded, "Yeah, I whined complained and protested, but she said you'd threatened to kill me or something." She said.

Adam said, "That was a lie to shut you up."

Adam then explained what had happened in the time they'd been away except the parts about killing by the time he finished explaining it was afternoon. She hugged him, crying, and held him tightly.

Christina said, "I c-can't believe all this time you loved me, and when my parents found out they kept us apart."

Adam nodded and said, "If you don't feel that way about me, I understand, but I desperately need a friend.

"I am sure my other friends' parents told them a similar lie when they found out I went to Cortez PAU.

"Also, if you are tired of living with them as I was sick of living with my parents, please stay with me so we can both finally be happy together.

"I have the means to take care of us both, I promise."

Christina nodded, smiling, "Adam, you have been my best friend who wasn't female.

"My parents pushed me so hard to study so I could be better than you.

"The truth is, I really liked you just as you were and wanted us to be friends forever if not more than that."

Adam blushed, and the two of them leaned in for their first kiss. They both blushed and felt vibrations throughout their bodies.

Adam said, "I feel funny in my tummy."

Christina laughed and said, "Me too."

Adam blushed a lot, "H-hey um Christina?"

"Yeah?" she responded, looking at him.

Adam continued, "Well, your parents probably sent out people to look for you, so I was wondering if there was anything you wanted to do before we have to run from here?"

She laughed and said, "Well, I remember one time in the pool, you discretely flashed your junk at me when my mom wasn't looking."

Adam blushed again and said, "I-I can't believe you remember that we were like seven, then, right?"

She laughed harder, practically rolling on the bed with laughter.

Adam smiled, "Well, I have a confession to make. I am a cat boy."

Adam pulled out his two tails and his cat ears.

Christina looked horrified.

"Y-you are the one the police are looking for!" she said.

Adam nodded and said, "Yes, because of me, approximately five thousand five hundred seventy people between 'Cortez PAU Lark Ellen and Cypresses Clothes Are Fashionable' are gone, not to mention some mental hospital patients.

"I wasn't myself when I did it the book of necromancy.

"It took over my mind for that time I swear it's true."

She shivered in fear as if she was staring death in the face.

"I-I hate you!" she said.

She ran to the door and tried to escape.

Adam was sobbing uncontrollably, "Please don't go!

"Please don't leave!

"Please don't leave me!

"You are the only one I still care about in this world.

"If I lose you, I have nothing!" he cried.

She banged on the door and forced it open Adam chased her through Covina. He grabbed her by the pant legs, which she kicked off to get away from him. She had a panda face on her panties. Christina shouted, "Leave me alone, damn it! I don't want to be with you anymore!" It was at this moment volunteer police officer Steve Adam's former next-door neighbor arrived with the audiotape from the Charter Oak Mental Hospital that Adam left behind.

"Enough is enough Adam you are wanted in connection with the disappearances of countless individuals and now lewd behavior.

"You have the right to remain silent.

"Anything you say can and will be used against you in a court of law.

"You have the right to speak with an attorney and to have an attorney present during any and all questioning, and if you cannot afford one, you will be provided with one at government expense!"

Before Adam could react, several officers tackled Adam to the ground and arrested him. He clung to the book of necromancy for dear life within his grim reaper cloak. Adam and Christina were taken to the Covina Police and Fire Station for questioning since it was nearby and was only recently abandoned.

Heidi Major brought in some bagels and donuts for the questioning room, and Sarah was waving her finger at him while Scott just shook his head. Christina was questioned in a separate room. Her parents and Adam's were called, and none too pleased with Adam at all. They both stared daggers into his questioning room.

Steve asked Adam, "Why, Adam, why did you do it?

"Why did you stay in Covina, and why did you cause your former age mates to disappear, and more importantly, how?"

Joanne and David were also ticked off at Adam, but they were the only two that Adam loved too much to kill besides maybe Christina but a different kind of love.

Adam replied, "The Book of Necromancy

He pulled it out.

"When I opened it up, I felt a brand-new power surge within me, and then suddenly, my body felt like it was acting on instinct; my thoughts soon became my actions."

Steve said, "So that castle where Cortez PAU once stood is yours?"

Adam nodded and said, "Good luck, proving I did any of this in court.

"I doubt the law has anything on what I've done.

"I will probably be let off the hook because there is no concrete evidence to suggest necromancy even exists.

"Go ahead and open it if you want to see if it works."

Steve cautiously opened the book, and it began sucking both Steve and any other officers in the room inside it through what appeared to be a portal hole in the book. Once inside, they battled for their lives against endless waves of tortured souls.

Adam closed the book trapping them inside. "How unusual it seems if anyone but the one who commands the dead within this book opens it, they get trapped inside."

Adam gave the book to Heidi Major, and she turned the page. Officers rushed to try to pull her out as did Heidi Clauss, Mr. Clauss, and Scott and Sarah Major, but they all got sucked in. Now only Joanne and David and Christina remained in the office.

A beeping sound was heard from David's paw. After examining it, he took Joanne with him and ran out of town. Adam let them go because he still cared about them. He then walked over to Christina.

Christina said, "Adam, stop it.

"Haven't you killed enough people already?"

Adam replied, "I am not here to kill you.

"I could never because I love you why can't you accept that?"

Christina replied, "Because you are a monster, a freak of nature, and you made my parents disappear!

"Meanwhile, Cathy is now all alone with no one to care for her.

"She'll soon starve to death if you don't kill her first."

Adam flipped through his book of necromancy and found a spell to allow him to erase her memories of this day and only remember him for the person he used to be. He used it.

Her eyes dilated and glowed a red color as the spell was cast. She forgot the events that happened that day or so Adam thought and went home with her to his castle room. It was the early evening after all the questioning and actions that occurred. Once inside, he pulled off his cloak being in nothing but cargo shorts and underwear beneath it. They went onto his bed.

12 A HAPPY ENDING?

Do not Read This Part If You Are Under Eighteen, You Have Been Warned

Christina blushed, "Um Adam, why am I in my panties except for my shirt?"

Adam said, "Uh, I think you were going to play dress-up with me or something."

"Oh," she said.

Christina laughed and nuzzled Adam.

"You know I've never seen a cat person before, but you are incredibly cute with those two tails and ears of yours."

She rubbed both his ears and his two tails, causing him to purr uncontrollably.

This only made her squeal with delight as she loved cats a lot.

Adam said, "Um Christina, please refrain from doing that."

He had a bulge in his pants. Christina giggled cutely and pulled off his cargo shorts and revealed his cute kitten boxers.

"Aww, even your underwear is adorable!" She said with delight.

Adam blushed redder. His two tails formed a heart shape, and his Star of David pendant shifted colors between a red tint to resemble love and a purple one to indicate lust.

Christina didn't notice that her shirt had lifted almost halfway, exposing her belly button while she was rolling around on the bed. Her belly button was small, and rather than stick out like a nipple, it was one you could stick your finger into just like Adam's. Adam looked at it with a blush on his face. The temptation to give it a poke was more than he could resist because he'd kissed her not more than a few hours ago tops.

Christina laughed loudly when he touched it.

"Stop that you are tickling me!" she said.

Her face was redder from blushing. She, like Adam, slept in bed barefoot. Thus, when she laughed, he couldn't help noticing she would kick her bare feet. He curled up at them and nuzzled them with his nose, causing her to laugh and accidentally kick him in the face with them, which rather than piss him off instead turned him on oddly enough.

Adam blushed and said, "D-do that again, please, it felt good."

Christina seemed confused, "You want me to do what Adam?"

Adam responded, "Lightly put your feet on my face as if kicking me but not enough to hurt me more like you are stepping on me."

Christina tilted her head and said, "Um Adam…

"You are acting rather strangely.

"Are you feeling, ok?"

Adam smiled and said, "Yeah, I just think you are utterly adorable…

"It's like ordinarily, I am afraid to show emotion these days.

"But when I am with you, I get this weird feeling in my tummy.

"I always did since we were little."

Christina giggled a little, "Is that why you always used to make those cute sighing sounds when I turned my back?"

Adam blushed, "I can't believe you remember that, but yes."

He remembered that in erasing her memory of her discovering what he'd done to Covina and West Covina, she probably forgot they had their first kiss that night.

"Um Christina?" he asked.

Christina responded, "Yeah?"

Adam replied, "Well, um, I think I am in love with you and would like you to be the first one I ever kiss."

She blushed, remembering all the Disney fairy tales they used to watch together during the times she would visit him throughout his younger years. She remembered that most of them ended with the boy and girl or man and woman kissing and living happily ever after.

Christina "So this is the happily ever after of our lives?"

Adam shook his head, "I wouldn't say this is the end of our story not yet anyway but rather the beginning of something much more significant.

"You see, there is more to the story that is lazily ended with 'and they lived happily ever after' that the reader or viewer never sees."

Christina leaned in and kissed him on the lips taking him a bit by surprise at how spontaneous it was.

Christina said, "I feel funny in my tummy."

Adam replied "That my friend or I guess my girlfriend now is called 'love.'"

Christina sighed happily. "It feels good, Adam, it really does.

"My body is getting a bit hot, so maybe we want to get out of the blankets."

Adam nodded, and both of them got on top of the bedsheets.

"Hey Christina, do you think since I am well as you know part kitty, I could maybe act like one and lick you?"

She laughed in response and said, "Sure, Adam."

Adam began licking her belly button, causing her to roll around with laughter. Adam meowed like a kitty as he did.

"Hey, um Adam?" asked Christina.

Adam asked, "Yeah?"

"Well, I was wondering if you could tell me something.

"I never thought of it much before, but I remember the time we were at the swimming pool, and I was in my one-piece, but your swimsuit only covered your waist."

Adam nodded

"What about it?" he asked.

Christina said, "Well, I have read many books, but my mommy never told me why girl's swimsuits were so different than boys."

Adam smiled; his face was still red from a blush.

He said, "Well, with boys when we mature, I've read they don't produce milk in our nipples except under peculiar conditions.

"So, the swimsuits that cover nearly every inch of you are training you to always hide your nipples.

"This is because one day, they will become breasts with which to feed babies.

"Our society, for this reason, considers them sexual things even though their purpose is far nobler than they are treated if we are to assume life is just."

Christina had a noticeable blush on her face as she thought about that for a few moments.

"Is that why you've been staring at my chest and tummy the whole time you explained that?"

Adam realized he was staring lovingly at them at that moment and blushed.

"I guess so.

"I didn't know I was a boy until I accidentally saw my mom come out of the shower because I knew nothing about gender features." He said.

Christina replied, "I think that is the thing I admired most about you.

"The fact that you weren't like the other immature boys who were afraid to admit their feelings."

Adam said, "I admired that you were one of the few people I knew who could understand some of the more complicated things I said.

"You always had an answer rather than just a puzzled expression.

"I could tell you had a genuine desire to understand the world as I did.

"I think we were made for each other."

She nodded in agreement and looked down to notice her shirt was halfway up.

Christina tugged at it teasingly as if to ask, "Want me to take it off?"

Adam nodded, blushing.

She slowly pulled her shirt off as Adam's pupils dilated, indicating he liked what he saw, and his pendant stayed purple shining as she did.

"T-They are cute mew. C- can I-I touch?" He blurted out in the heat of the moment.

Adam's body was quivering with a combination of nervousness as he'd never had a girl willingly show him her nipples and excitement. His penis felt like it was going to burst through his boxers.

Christina smiled innocently and nodded. Adam reached his hand to her and gently poked her button-like nipples, which caused her to laugh because it tickled and tingled for him to touch them. As a result of the drafts that occasionally blew in through his castle and the attention, her nipples got bumpy and erect. Adam smiled.

"Even though they aren't as oval as adult's breasts, they are fun to poke mew."

Christina smiled and grabbed his head, rubbing his cat ears against her nipples. Adam traced circles around her nipples with his fingertips causing her to let out a cute moan while laughing. She gave him a hug and pressed her little female nipples against his male ones.

"This is the best hug I've ever had!" Adam said.

Christina said, "I feel tingly in my panties and well like I peed myself, but it doesn't smell like urine."

Adam looked down at her panties. They were soaked from all the love he's given her up to this point.

Adam said, "When a female wants to make a baby with a male, her vagina will get wet and open up to invite the boy to comfortably stick his penis inside it.

"This is what foreplay, that is, sexual touching, rubbing, and licking, is supposed to accomplish across various erogenous zones.

"Erogenous zones are body parts that whether society deems them private parts or not would stimulate this tingly feeling you feel that is making your panties soaked."

She smirked and put her foot on his face "Start licking kitty they are dirty and need a cleaning."

Adam blushed and did as she commanded, surprised a bit by her sudden shift in attitude. He did as she commanded, cleaning her bare feet, and she was laughing the entire time and practically purple in the face by the time he finished.

"Good job, my pet now for your reward."

She kissed his male nipples causing him to blush a bit and his nipples to harden from the stimulus if the occasional cold drafts through his castle hadn't already. She laid on her back, pointing to her nipples.

"Show me how these will feed babies, please." She begged.

Adam nodded, and he pressed his tongue upon her nipples in circles and up and down. She continued to moan louder and louder while laughing because it tickled and tingled.

Christina said, "A-Adam p- please t-this is g-good b-but my vagina it's leaking so much."

Adam was sucking on her nipples at that moment like a baby. He was so focused on sucking on her nipples that he failed to notice his own boxers were almost as soaked as her panties. She pulled him away and pulled down his boxers, revealing his kitty penis with barbs on it. She licked the tip of it, causing Adam to lay back and moan and purr loudly. Her licking quickly turned into sucking, and Adam continued moaning louder and louder.

"C-Christina t-that f-feels s-so g-good!" he mewled in pleasure.

Her breath and mouth upon his shaft were like a hot and humid summer day. His penis felt like an exotic hard candy in her mouth. The barbs were like if someone licked and stuck cat claws to a person's penis. Adam was still a virgin, so he ejaculated in her mouth with little effort.

Adam screamed a bit in pain as his penis felt as though someone jabbed a toothpick through the pee hole or hammered a nail into it as is typical for the first time a male ever ejaculates.

"Meow!" he moaned in a mix of pain and pleasure.

Christina asked, "Are you ok, Adam?"

Adam nodded, "Yeah, I am just in a bit of pain as my penis isn't used to ejaculation yet."

Christina smiled.

"Don't worry, we can fix that."

Adam replied with a smirk, "Well, give it a few moments to rest and maybe lick it a bit more to help it heal."

She touched the tip of his penis with her tongue. His two tails stretched underneath his crotch and pulled down her panties, exposing her virgin vaginal slit complete with labia, urethra, and clitoris, all of which were dripping orgasm fluids. His two tails went under her one went in her vagina hole, and the other went in her rear end. This caused her to let out a loud yelp.

"Are you ok?" asked Adam.

She nodded, "You just took me by surprise."

He slowly slid them in and out of the two holes, the fur tickling the inside of both holes while delivering unimaginable pleasure. Christina moaned as she was licking Adam's tip.

"A-Adam, I want you to have my virginity.

"Stick your kitty penis in me.

"I want to bear your kittens!" she mewled.

Adam nodded and took the tail that was in her vagina out and licked it.

"You taste good." He mewed.

He stuck his prickly cat penis into her vagina, causing her to scream in a mix of pain and pleasure because barbed cat penises hurt as well as feel good no matter how many times one uses them. In and out, he thrust his penis into her vagina, and his tail in her rear end up it.

"It hurts! But I like it." Christina mewled.

He broke through her hymen, which caused his penis to get bloody, and she screamed in a mix of pain and pleasure. Her body quivered with the pleasure she was receiving and from the sensation of having her hymen burst. Her vagina lips were giving his penis a bear hug. He continued to penetrate her in and out, moaning in unison with her with pleasure. He finally ejaculated into her and retracted his catlike penis.

13 THE BOOK OF DEMONOLOGY

Confession Time

Adam panted, "Wow, that was simply amazing Christina I never felt so good in my entire life!"

Christina was also panting, "Yeah, I never thought I would ever feel this good in my life.

"I have a confession to make, though."

"What is it?"

"I may be human, but I also came into possession of a similar book to yours called 'The Book of Demonology.'

"As with your book of necromancy, it can control both demons and undead."

Adam scratched his head in confusion, "So that spell I used to try to make you forget, did it work?"

Christina shook her head, "No, it didn't.

"I was afraid you'd kill me for being human and hurting you by not calling anymore since all the ones you killed had hurt you in some way.

"You see, I secretly loved you too much to kill you but, just the thought you'd misuse this power, not for self-defense but revenge was overwhelming.

"When you used the spell, I knew you weren't going to kill me.

"I knew if you wanted to, you would have already."

"If you can control demons as well as I manage dead things, why would I be able to kill you?

"Also, don't our books have the same powers essentially?"

Christina Shook her head, "No, they do not have the same powers.

"Also, I am not an expert when it comes to commanding them as you are.

"So, while our abilities may be equal in strength, either of us can kill the other with the proper strategy.

"Necromancers although they control demons as well mainly focus on the demonic spirits rather than the physical kind associated with Hell.

"That is, according to my 'Book of Demonology', not all demons are dead.

"Some are born out of hatred in people's hearts or by procreation with other demons.

"Those are the kind I command for the most part, but because there are such things as demonic spirits, I can also give those bodies and summon them."

Adam was amazed, "So you are telling me that my variant allows me to control zombies ghosts demonic spirits, and yours enables you to control demonic spirits and any demons you want?"

Christina nodded, "Precisely, your powers are mainly based on things that have passed away mine are based on things that have evil intent.

"You could say that comparing our abilities is like comparing apples to oranges."

Adam smiled, "So I am not alone after all!"

"Yes, I basically pretended to forget so you wouldn't try to kill me."

"I knew you loved me when you attempted to erase my memory, so I played along.

"Also, even though I didn't have the tragic life you did, I too found my book quite by accident."

"Go on," Adam replied.

"As I was saying, I was in the library, studying as my mom commanded when I happened upon a strange book written in Latin.

"I spent hours trying to translate the cover, and it turned out it said 'Book of Demonology-Do Not Open.'

"I didn't believe it, but curiosity got the better of me, so I turned to the first page of it, and the same thing that happened to you happened to me."

Adam seemed puzzled and said, "But I thought books like these are only found by those who were living tragically hard lives.

"If this is correct, then it explains how I happened to find mine and was able to use it."

Christina said, "Only a Kabbalist or real love could send either of our powers back if we wanted to send them back.

"As for why it chose me, I would guess that these books favor those with extraordinary qualities, whether it is an intellectual gift or hatred and a desire for vengeance.

"The latter of which makes sense for you because undead is thought to be spirits that couldn't pass on into the afterlife.

"They take the form of ghosts or zombies, among others, while demons can vary in what drives them to exist.

"I may never know exactly how I fit the criteria to hold the opposite book to yours, but the fact remains I do."

Adam pondered it for a while and then fell asleep, snuggling Christina. Christina smiled and slept with him.

Several Months Later, Adam Birthed the babies Christina was pregnant with. Christina birthed quadruplets consisting of two girls and two boys. The firstborn son was named "Adam" and was given the suffix "Jr." the firstborn daughter was named "Eve." The second-born son was named "Noah," and the second-born daughter was named "Naomi."

Adam and Christina vowed to take care of them as long as they lived. The Abandoned stores had many goods more than Adam or Christina could ever use. So, any excess products were taken to market to be sold by Christina, and she did the shopping for the family members of the human race that survived, thus far, still didn't believe in magic or supernatural as a reliable means of convicting criminals. As such, they were unable to prove what Adam did in court or that he existed. Adam, Christina, and the rest of the family remained in isolation from the remainder of the world. That is except for the shopping trips that Christina made. Because Christina was human and able to trade with other humans, they successfully created a place where hybrids could live in secrecy without hiding their identity from people within the sanctuary. Adam's Mom and Dad continued to live among humans incognito and never made contact with Adam from this point on. Despite this, Adam, Christina, Adam Jr, Eve, Noah, and Naomi lived happily ever after!

THE END!

ABOUT THE AUTHOR

Adam Thomas Applebaum has an Associate in Applied Sciences Degree in Computer Information Systems. His backstory is one only his trusted friends will ever know in full unless he publishes an Autobiography of it. He wrote books like this one and was a tutor for children in a variety of subjects if the kids were high school level and below.

Please Contact Me

Phone: 310-561-6330
Email: adam.applebaum1@gmail.com
Or
Adam T Applebaum
PO Box 14606
Torrance, CA 90503

To further support my Efforts

Author Website:
https://www.theforsakenscribe.com/

Subscribe to Me on YouTube:
http://www.youtube.com/user/AdathorRules